A BOOK IS A NEW ADVENTURE

Emily D.

BPO-35939 © 2003 Antioch Publishing

To Matouš and Lukáš

First U.S. edition 2008

Library of Congress Cataloging-in-Publication Data is available
Library of Congress Catalog Card Number: 2007938324

2 4 6 8 10 9 7 5 3 1

Printed in China

This book was typeset in Futura Light.
The illustrations were done in mixed media.

Candlewick Press
2067 Massachusetts Avenue
Cambridge, Massachusetts 02140

visit us at www.candlewick.com

CANDLEWICK PRESS
CAMBRIDGE, MASSACHUSETTS

Honk

Look Out, Suzy Goose

Petr Horáček

It was a beautiful afternoon.

All the geese were honking . . .

except for Suzy Goose.

How **NOISY** it is here, thought Suzy.

I wish I could find a quiet place.

The woods looked quiet.

FLIP,

FLOP,

So off she went.

FLIP,
FLOP.

FLIP, FLOP, FLIP, FLOP.

Peace and quiet, thought Suzy.
It's nice to be alone.

But Suzy Goose was **not** alone.

TIPTOE, TIPTOE,

padded the hungry fox.

"I spy goose for dinner."

He followed Suzy into the woods.

FLIP, FLOP, FLIP, FLOP.

FLIP,
FLOP,
FLIP,
FLOP.

"I feel so much better
now that I'm alone," said Suzy.
But Suzy Goose was **not** alone,
and the fox was hungry.
A wolf spied them both.

CREEP,
CREEP.

"I spy fox and goose,"
whispered the wolf.

TIPTOE, TIPTOE.

FLIP, FLOP,

FLIP, FLOP,

"Mmm.
Goose for dinner,"
murmured the fox.   went Suzy Goose.

Deeper
into the woods
they went.
A huge bear
watched
them pass.

"I spy a
delicious
dinner,"
he growled.
"Wolf, fox,
AND goose!"

FLIP,
FLOP,
FLIP,
FLOP

PAD,
PAD,
went the
bear.

CREEP,
CREEP,
sneaked
the wolf.

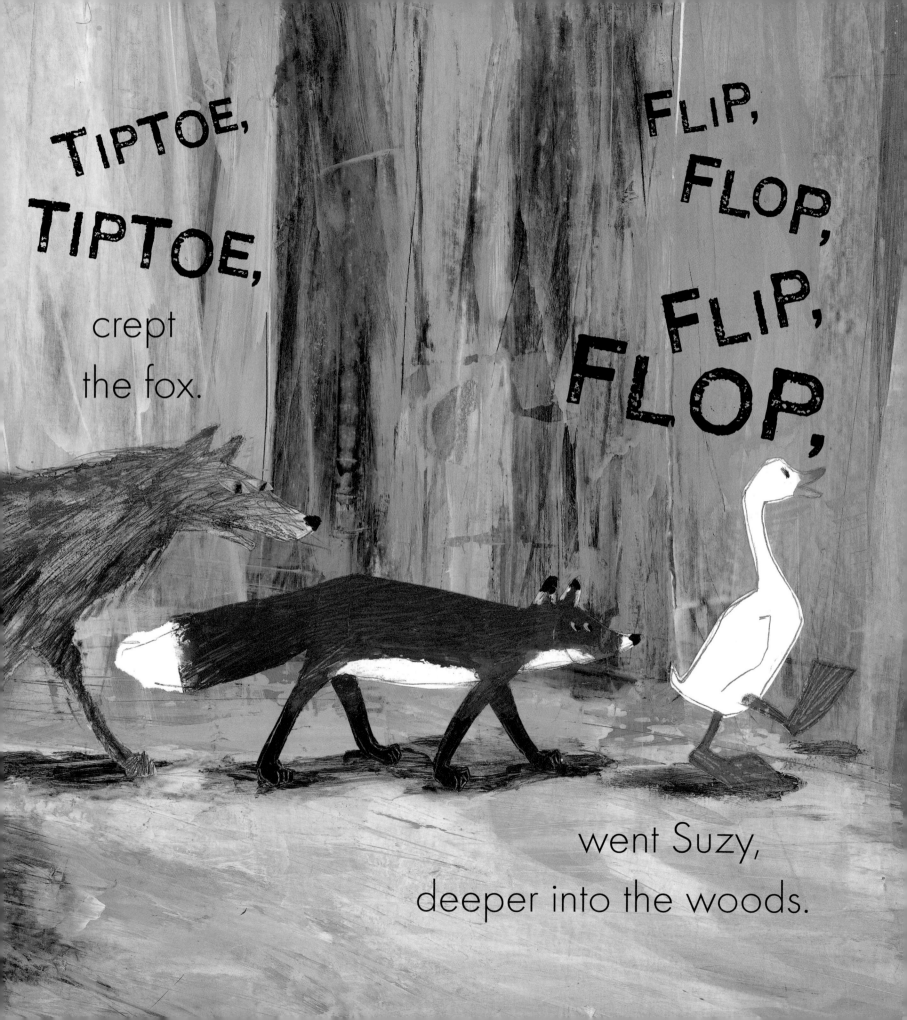

At last she reached a clearing.

It was very quiet.

Suzy stopped
and looked up.

She was so happy,
she let out a very loud **HONK.**
The noise woke up
the old owl.

Everybody **ran**.

Suzy ducked. What a racket!

She looked around,
but she didn't see anybody.
What was that **NOISE**? she thought.
It's scary being here by myself.

And she hurried back home.

FLIP, FLOP,

It was good to be
back with her flock.

And it was nice and quiet.